The Rabbi Who Flew

Written and Illustrated by

Renate Dollinger

A Grandma Hanne Sheyne Story

Booksmythe

LOS ANGELES

Requests for permission should be mailed to:
Booksmythe,
17216 Saticoy St., # 360
Van Nuys, CA 91406

Library of Congress Card Number: 00-107482
Dollinger, Renate R., 1924–
The Rabbi Who Flew/by Renate Dollinger
            p.   cm
                Summary:
A rabbi prays so deeply that he flies, but the village shoemaker
realizes that he must secretly repair the rabbi's shoes so that
nobody sees the holes in his shoes when he flies over them.
                ISBN 0-945585-20-9

10 9 8 7 6 5 4 3 2 1

Printed in Hong Kong

*To my wonderful family and
to my ever helpful Rabbi Ellison.*

It was again such a beautiful autumn day. The trees were full of red and yellow leaves—the bushes also had ripe, red berries. Grandma Hanne Sheyne (*Hah-neh Shay-neh*) poured herself a cup of tea and sat down on her favorite rocking chair. Her warm, brown eyes laughed with delight when she looked at all the children in her house. She gave a happy sigh and called to them, "Come here! Let me tell you the tale about a special rabbi who prayed so deeply that he flew!"

There was a tiny town, as small as a village, called Gill. Those little towns were called *shtetls*. They were home to the Jewish people of all kinds—big and little, pretty and plain, young and old, *and* poor and very poor. Gill had tailors, bakers, one shoemaker, candlemakers, milkmen, and THE SWEETEST RABBI that was ever born; a truly holy man named Rabbi Frum.

In this shtetl there also lived two boys, Yankel and Moshe who were nine years old. They went to *heder* (school) together ever since they were little boys. In *heder* they learned to read the *aleph-bess* (alphabet), to pray, and the stories of the *Torah* (Five Books of Moses). Yankel and Moshe didn't like heder very much because the *melamed* (teacher) yelled a lot. But when Rabbi Frum came he brought them candy and would quietly tell the *melamed* not to yell. The *rebbe* (Rabbi Frum) would tell the best stories from the Bible about wild animals, fierce battles, mighty kings, and great miracles. Everyone loved him.

On Friday evening and during the day on Saturday everybody went to the one and only *shul* (synagogue) for *Shabbes* (Sabbath). There were also morning and afternoon services, but usually only the boys' papas attended them. The Jews have many holy days—so Rabbi Frum was very busy in the shul leading the services and the entire congregation with his gentle hand.

One fine Shabbes morning, Yankel and Moshe, who stood in the front of the shul, noticed something strange. They were watching the rebbe, swaying sideways and bobbing up and down while he prayed. He always did that, but this time, as he sang to the Lord, he would rise off the ground a little bit every now and then. Both boys were transfixed. As the morning went on, Rabbi Frum lifted a bit higher all the time. Nobody else noticed anything.

Yankel and Moshe talked about it all week, but they didn't tell anybody else about it. Next Shabbes they couldn't wait to go to shul. In the middle of the morning, Moshe nudged Yankel and pointed at Rabbi Frum. HE WAS LIFTING AGAIN! This time a little higher. And lo and behold, still higher and higher. Pretty soon other people started to notice. His eyes were closed as he *davened* (prayed) with a gentle hum. He began floating a little forward and a little backward, to and fro, forwards and backwards, and sometimes even side to side. There was a hush. People almost stopped breathing—what if he fell? He might break, *oy vey*, maybe break a hip. But with the last prayer Rabbi Frum slowly descended and said, "Amen."

Quietly the congregation went out of the shul. They stood outside in the sunshine and looked at each other in amazement. Reb Lumpy, the butcher said, "A MIRACLE!"

The story spread like wildfire. The next town, Polsk,

heard all about it. Such stories! All the ladies in the area

talked about it all the time.

By the next Shabbes families from Polsk had arrived and the little shul in Gill was very full. All the seats were taken so people stood in the back, and people even stood outside looking through the windows. Such excitement; everybody was waiting for the rebbe to fly!

When the service started you could hear a pin drop. The prayers started and the men began to sway right to left as they prayed. Pretty soon Rabbi Frum lifted a little bit. Just a little bit. Then the Lord's spirit entered his heart and he lifted more and more. Within twenty minutes he flew over the congregation. Back and forth from one end to the other. From the wall in the front to the wall in the back. The Jews from Gill and Jews from Polsk were struck silent in awe. The women cried quietly in joy—such wonder! In the meantime the rebbe, puzzled by all the hullabaloo, kept flying. He did the whole service right to the ending prayer, *Adon Olam*, and slowly descended.

The families went home for Shabbes dinner. Over chicken soup with noodles, the shoemaker was telling his family, one wife, four children—all beautiful, may they live to one hundred and twenty— "The rebbe's shoes are not right."

"What's wrong with them," asked his wife, Beyla?

"The rebbe has holes in the soles of his shoes," he answered. "Everybody can see it. Maybe not yet, but they will. What will they think of our town? What will they think of me? Here, I am the shoemaker of Gill, and our wonderful rebbe has holes in his shoes."

Beyla looked at her husband with alarm. "What can we do? We cannot tell him, he will be so embarrassed. And to shame that holy rebbe would be a mortal SIN." They talked all afternoon and then Moshe, the youngest boy in the family who was nine years old, stood up and said, "Papa, measure his shoes as he flies by you. Tomorrow morning take a measuring stick to shul and hold it up and measure his sole as he flies over you." What a brilliant idea! They lifted Moshe up and danced him round and round the table.

The next day was beautiful; the sky was bright blue and the birds were singing. The shoemaker was at the shul early. He was ever so excited. His heart went pounding, clip-clop, clip-clop. In his sleeve was the measuring stick. He went to sit right in the center of the congregation. About the middle of the morning the rebbe started lifting and soon was flying. Out of his sleeve Reb Finkel took the measuring stick and as the rebbe's feet went over his head he held the stick up in the air. The rebbe flew by several times before he got all the measurements.

As soon as the service was over Reb Finkel went home and started making the new soles. But how could they get the rebbe's shoes without him knowing it? Ah—Moshe would have to go to the rebbe's house in the night and fetch the shoes. They would have to be mended overnight.

On Tuesday night—the moon was out—Moshe left to sneak into the rebbe's house and find his shoes. There was our sweet rebbe asleep in bed with his shoes right by the bed. Moshe grabbed them and quiet as a mouse he crept out the door. He never knew that the rebbe was peeking.

Everybody at home was eagerly waiting for him to get back.

Well, thought Reb Finkel, I will fix them completely and give my

rebbe shoes that are done right. All night, the shoemaker, Reb

Finkel, worked on those shoes finishing just before dawn.

Moshe looked at the shoes and said, "Good job, Papa. They

look new."

The cock was crowing and Moshe left to bring the shoes back. Ever so quietly he opened the door to the rebbe's house. All was silent. Moshe looked at the rebbe to make sure that he was still asleep. Just then the rebbe moved and Moshe froze in place. Rabbi Frum wanted to laugh but just snored so that the boy would think he was asleep. Finally, Moshe put the shoes back just the way he found them and went home. Moshe was very proud that he snuck in and out twice without being noticed. After Moshe left, Rabbi Frum chuckled and said a blessing for the boy and his family.

Next Shabbes the shul was filled to overflowing with people standing outside looking in the windows. Prayers started and there was a rumbling and mumbling as everybody was praying with all their hearts. Nine o'clock then ten o'clock—Moshe was waiting. "There he goes," he said to Yankel. Up went the *rebbe*! A little up, a lot up, more, and he flew. Oh, heavenly blessings! The shoemaker sang *"Baruch Ha Shem*—Blessed be his Name" as the *rebbe* sailed by, flying higher than ever before. Looking up at his shiny shoes with two brand new soles, Reb Finkel was ever so happy.

When the congregation finished morning service he and Moshe
went home to hallah, chicken soup with noodles, chicken and
sweet carrots, and honey cake for dessert. Moshe turned to his
father and said, "Good job, Papa!" Reb Finkel hugged his son
and said, "Good job, Moshe!"

Renate Dollinger is well-known as a Jewish expressionist whose paintings and intaglio prints are widely shown and collected throughout the United States and Canada. Whether referred to as a "Jewish Bruegel," "Grandma Moses of the shtetl," or as a "pictorial storyteller of the Jewish world," she is known worldwide for vivid, wonderful paintings that depict village life with humor and warmth.

Routinely working in media ranging from oil to ink, these illustrations were done in gouache and enhanced with pen and ink. The text was set using the Tiepolo family of fonts. This book was printed and bound in Hong Kong by Pacific Rim International Printing on 100# Neo Art gloss stock and case-bound with a smythe-sewn, hardcover library binding.